Princess Daisy

written by Diane Grabow illustrated by Betty Stears

ISBN-13: 978-1456461010

To Princesses of all ages and to my beautiful Mother.-D.G.

To my daughter's imagination and the challenge this book created for me to reach for the painted stars in the sky.-B.S.

Special thanks to the Princes in our life: Chuck, Mike, Matt, and Juel for their support, encouragement, and enduring take-out while we worked on this book. And Dave A. for editing and overall advice over many cups of coffee.

There once lived a pretty pink English Daisy.

She lived on a farm where the chores drove her crazy.

She thought you could tell by her beautiful face,

She was far too special for this common place.

She was convinced a mistake must have been made.

She belonged in a castle with a butler and maid.

She'd sip bottled water while she sat in the shade.

Instead of weeding and watching the babies while they

played.

One day in frustration she loudly proclaimed,

"From now on, Princess is my name!"

The flowers agreed to what she had to say.

There was no use in arguing. She always got her way.

The wise old sunflower looked down at her.

Princess crossly said, "You're in my way Sir!"

He replied, "There's lots of sunshine to share."

She snapped back, "I'm a princess; it's not fair!"

Later that day, the sun was high in the sky.

The babies were thirsty and started to cry.

Princess gave them her last drops of saved rain.

"I'm thirsty too," she said, "but I don't complain."

Taking care of the babies was a pain!

All of this sharing was a terrible drain.

Princess decided she had to be free.

So she made plans for when she would flee.

That night, the flowers were tucked in the garden bed.

The sunflower snored loudly as he bowed his head.

The babies had whined about going to sleep.

But when she checked on them, they didn't make a

peep.

While they were all dreaming of sunny weather,

She dug-up and gathered her roots together.

Gazing at the stars above, she plotted her course.

And with one last look back, she left without remorse.

She walked on her long roots through the dark night.

The full moon above was her only light.

After a few hours, her roots were wilted and dried out.

When she saw the ocean ahead, she gave a happy shout!

The beach was empty up-and-down the shore.

There was no one to share with anymore.

Princess planted her roots in the soft sand.

The waves lulled her to a peaceful dreamland.

She was asleep when she heard a loud sound.

Princess was shocked as she looked all around.

The beach was full of people packed everywhere.

They sat on bright towels or on lawn chairs.

By noon, her pink petals had started to fade.

There weren't any trees to provide cool shade.

The beach was too crowded she started to think.

And the ocean was much too salty to drink.

By nightfall, she was thirsty and tired.

Princess wasn't sure what she desired.

She was so exhausted, but couldn't get to sleep.

Tears rolled down her face as she started to weep.

She realized taking care of the babies wasn't so bad.

And never seeing them again made her feel sad.

She missed the farm, she realized with fright.

And the stars above didn't seem so shiny and bright.

Princess was tired of being alone.

She yelled at the moon, "I want to go home!"

Her trip had been an unhappy pursuit.

So she reached down and pulled-up her dry roots.

She shook off her roots and headed home fast.

Over hills and through valleys she flew past.

She was so happy when the babies came into sight.

Princess scooped them up and hugged them tight.

The babies had missed her; they weren't even mad.

Even the wise old sunflower seemed glad.

"I'm sorry I was so bossy," she confessed.

"I guess I'm not a real princess."

But the babies cried, "It just isn't true."

"You're special to us," and "We love you!"

For the babies had known it from the start.

She had always been a princess in her heart.

The End

Diane and Betty are a Mother-Daughter writing and illustrating team. They live in Boise, Idaho.

They are currently working on their second book, Mortimer's Midnight Mishap, the tall tale of a tiny mouse.

Diane has been writing stories since her first creative writing class in 3rd grade. She also enjoys interior decorating and has an antique booth where she sells all sorts of cute treasures.

Betty has been hooked on art since her first messy finger painting lesson in first grade. She paints and draws in all mediums. She loves to have fun and enjoy life.

To Jeff Smart
life is a journey
Enjoy ~ Betty Stoars
5/17/13 Enjoy life

18665943R00016

Made in the USA
Charleston, SC
15 April 2013